Enid Blyton's
NODDY
the Champion

BBC CHILDREN'S BOOKS

It was a lively morning in Toyland and Noddy was
training to take part in the Toyland Sports Day. He
was running around Toy Town but had to stop to catch
his breath.

"Good morning, Noddy," cried the Skittles as they ran past. They didn't look tired at all.

"I'm practising so hard, but I can't seem to run very fast," grumbled Noddy to himself. "I just can't. I need proper coaching from some clever person who'll cheer me up and tell me all the things I'm doing wrong."

At that very moment, Big-Ears cycled up. "I thought you'd be practising for the Sports Day," he said.

"Will you help me?" asked Noddy. "I can't seem to run very fast on my own."

"All right," agreed Big-Ears. "I'll be your coach."

Back at House-for-One, Noddy was running as fast as he could. "Come on, Noddy," cried Big-Ears, encouragingly. "Not far now!"

Noddy gasped to a halt. "Was I faster this time?" he panted. "Did I run a faster time on your stopwatch?"

Big-Ears looked embarrassed. "Er, I'm not sure. I'm afraid my stopwatch has stopped. Never mind – run round your house again. Cheer up!"

Just then, Master Tubby Bear ran up. "I've had such a good idea for the Sports Day," he said. "You and I could enter the three-legged race together."

"Don't be silly," replied Noddy. "We've only got two legs each."

"No, no," said Master Tubby. "We tie our legs together with my skipping rope. Then we'll have three legs! Big-Ears can coach us."

"That's a good idea," said Big-Ears. "Ready . . . steady . . . go!"

But Noddy and Master Tubby started to run off in different directions. They staggered, wobbled and fell right over.

"Ah!" said Big-Ears. "I see what you're doing wrong."

"I know what I'm doing wrong," said Noddy, crossly. "I shouldn't be running with Master Tubby. He messes up everything!"

"Ooh!" exclaimed Master Tubby, indignantly.

Just then, Tessie Bear came walking up the path. "Tessie!" cried Noddy. "Will you enter the three-legged race with me?"

"I can't," said Tessie Bear. "I've already promised to enter it with Dinah Doll. But you can borrow Bumpy Dog if you like."

"I came to see if you had any eggs," continued Tessie, "so that we could practise the egg-and-spoon race."

"Yes," said Noddy. "Big-Ears can be our coach."

Just then, they heard a loud "Hup!" from Mr Tubby Bear's garden, and saw him throwing a pillow into the air.

"He's been doing that all morning," said Master Tubby, "but he won't say why."

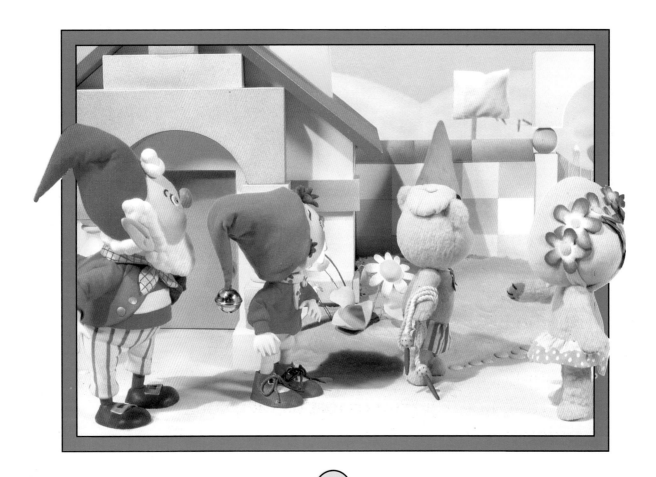

Eventually, they were all ready to practise the egg-and-spoon race. "On your marks . . . get set . . . go!" cried Big-Ears. Tessie and Master Tubby took off from the starting line, running as fast as they could without dropping the eggs.

Noddy, however, just stood at the line and threw his egg and spoon as far as he could. They sailed up into the air and then landed on the ground in front of him. He looked rather puzzled.

"Ah," said Big-Ears. "I see what you're doing wrong, Noddy. The eggs and spoons don't race on their own – you have to carry them along."

"I'm sorry," said Noddy. "I've never been in an egg-and-spoon race before."

"Never mind," said Big-Ears. "It'll be time to start the proper races soon. We'd better set off."

At the starting line, a crowd of toys were lined up. "Ladies and . . . erm . . . gentlemen," said Mr Plod, "the first event in the Toyland Sports Day will be the three-legged race. Ready, steady, go!"

Tessie Bear and Dinah Doll set off quickly and steadily, and were soon in the lead. Mr and Mrs Straw couldn't agree which leg should go first, and Martha Monkey and Master Tubby fell over at the finishing-line. Bumpy Dog was no help at all to Noddy as he just kept running round in circles. Tessie and Dinah won the race easily.

"Hurray!" cried all the watching toys.

The next event took place in Mr Straw's farmyard.

"Ladies and . . . erm . . . gentlemen," said Mr Plod, "may I have the first toy for the hay-bale tossing competition?"

"You have to toss the bale of hay as high as you can over the wall," explained Mr and Mrs Straw.

"It sounds easy to me," said Sammy Sailor, and he picked up the pitchfork and plunged it into the hay bale. He took a big swing and threw it as far as he could. It landed right next to the wall.

"May I be next?" asked Noddy.

Noddy picked up the hay bale,
but instead of throwing it over
the wall, he dropped it and
toppled over. Mr Straw's horse
thought it was very funny.
"Did I do something wrong?"
asked Noddy.

"The final contestant is Mr Tubby Bear," announced Mr Plod.

Mr Tubby took the pitchfork and tossed the bale of hay high up into the air. "Hup!" he cried, winning the contest easily.

"He's been practising!" said Noddy.

"So that's why he was throwing pillows about all morning!" exclaimed Big-Ears.

The next race was the hundred metres wobble, which Mr Wobbly Man won. In fact, he was the only one who entered it.

"Congratulations," said Mr Plod as he presented the prize. "And now to our final event – the grand egg-and-spoon race."

"I hope I win this," sighed Noddy. "I've not won anything yet."

   Everyone lined up at the start with their eggs and
spoons. "Take your marks . . . get set . . . go!" shouted
Mr Plod. Noddy tried to remember everything Big-Ears
had taught him about running.

"Come on! Faster, Clockwork Mouse!" called Mr Jumbo.
"I can't run any faster," said Clockwork Mouse. "I
forgot to wind up my clockwork." Mr Jumbo just shook
his head in despair.

"I say, Clockwork Clown," shouted Mr Tubby Bear, "you'll have to go faster than that, old fellow!" Poor Clockwork Clown was trying very hard to balance the egg on the spoon, but he wobbled forward too hard. The egg fell and smashed all over his face!

"Come on Noddy!" shouted Big-Ears. "You're in second place."

But Martha Monkey was running very fast indeed. She didn't seem to be worried at all about dropping her egg, and she charged across the finishing-line ahead of everyone else.

"I declare the winner to be Martha Monkey!"
announced Mr Plod.

"Hurray!" cried Martha, jumping up and down and
waving her arms in the air. She was still holding her egg
and spoon, and the egg didn't fall off.

"One moment, Miss Martha Monkey," said Mr Plod, sternly. "This egg will not come away from this spoon, which suggests, to my expert eye, that they are stuck together."

"Is there something wrong with that?" asked Martha, crossly.

"It's cheating!" said Mr Plod. "I'm afraid you're disqualified!'

"Come on, Noddy!" cried Big-Ears. "Come on!" Noddy ran as fast as he could and crossed the finishing-line in front of all the other runners.

"I declare the true winner of the egg-and-spoon race to be Noddy!" said Mr Plod.

"Well done, Noddy," said Big-Ears.

"It's all thanks to your coaching, Big-Ears," panted Noddy, breathlessly. He was delighted to have won a race at last.

"Ladies and . . . erm . . . everyone else," said Mr Plod. "As our only winner to have taken part in every single non-wobbling event, I declare Noddy to be the champion of the Sports Day!"

"Hurray!" cheered Big-Ears.

"Thank you, Mr Plod," said Noddy as he received the lovely silver trophy.

"Now I've got somewhere to put my egg," giggled Noddy, and he dropped his egg into the cup.

"Oh, good!" said Noddy. "Look! I've got scrambled eggs for tea."

"Hurray!" cheered the toys, laughing. "Hurray!"

Published by BBC Children's Books
a division of BBC Worldwide Limited
Woodlands, 80 Wood Lane, London W12 0TT

First published 1995

Text, stills & design copyright © 1995 BBC Children's Books

ISBN 0 563 40515 5

Based on the Television series, produced by Cosgrove Hall Films Limited,
inspired by the Noddy Books which are copyright © Darrell Waters Limited 1949-1968
Enid Blyton's signature and Noddy are trademarks of Darrell Waters Limited

Typeset in 17/21 pt Garamond by BBC Children's Books
Printed and bound in Great Britain by Cambus Litho, East Kilbride
Colour separations by DOT Gradations, Chelmsford
Cover printed by Cambus Litho, East Kilbride